*With deep gratitude and
appreciation for you ~
I give you this book as a gift
from my heart ~*

*Hear the gentle whisper of your
heart and be who you are meant
to be ~ compassionate love.*

GIVEN TO ~

RECEIVED FROM ~

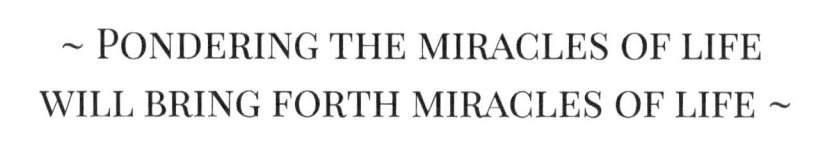

~ Pondering the miracles of life
will bring forth miracles of life ~

Ponder that you are a Miracle.

Books by
TRACY R. L. O'FLAHERTY

Loving Literature
LOVE from the Grand Universe
Series of Five Books

Book of Grace
Book of Compassion
Book of Kindness
Book of Inspiration
Book of Love

~

Through the Eyes of Finnan Frederick
Series of Three Novels
First Editions

I Love You Today ~ I Will Love You Tomorrow
I Love You Today ~ I Will Love You Always
I Love You Today ~ I Will Love You Forever

~

The Journey of Benevolence
Series of Three Books

Ease and Enlightenment
Wisdom and Enlightenment
Knowing and Enlightenment

~

Through the Eyes of Finnan Frederick
~ Special Edition ~
Complete ~ *I Love You* ~ Collection

Books by
TRACY R. L. O'FLAHERTY

The Journey of Benevolence
~ Special Edition ~
Complete ~ *Enlightenment* ~ Collection ~

~

LOVE from the Grand Universe
~ Wisdom from the Heavens ~ Collection ~

~

Good Heavens ~ Have You Found Your Twinkle?

~

Through the Eyes of Finnan Frederick
Series of Three Novels
Enhanced Editions

I Love You Today ~ I Will Love You Tomorrow
I Love You Today ~ I Will Love You Always
I Love You Today ~ I Will Love You Forever

~

A Journey of Wisdom as You Walk Upon Mother Earth

~

A Pathway of Wisdom as You Create Upon Mother Earth

~

Sharing a Study of Wisdom Brought Forth by You
~ *Wisdom Upon Mother Earth Series* ~
A Study Guide Accompanying
A Journey of Wisdom as You Walk Upon Mother Earth &
A Pathway of Wisdom as You Create Upon Mother Earth

Books by
TRACY R. L. O'FLAHERTY

Dad, Is That True?
Wisdom and Conversation from the Heavens

~

LOVE from the Grand Universe
~ Wisdom from the Heavens ~ Gift Book ~

~

Nigel and the Little Ones

~

The Truth Is... You Are Magnificent

~

A Birthday Book by Cheryl Elizabeth

~

The Tales of Tiernan
The Gift of a New Day

~

LOVE from the Grand Universe
Wisdom from the Heavens
~ Compassionate Compassion ~ Collection ~

~

The Truth Is...

You are Magnificent

TRACY R. L. O'FLAHERTY

Author

Tracy O'Flaherty

Book and Cover Design
TRACY R. L. O'FLAHERTY

* * *

Cover and Content Photographs taken by
TRACY R. L. O'FLAHERTY

* * *

© Copyright 2019
TRACY R. L. O'FLAHERTY
All Rights Reserved.

* * *

© Copyright 2018
Registration of Copyright
Canadian Intellectual Property Office
August 23, 2018
Umbrella Registration Number 1152333

As the Conversation Unfolds Series

Dad, Is That True?
Wisdom and Conversation from the Heavens
~
The Truth Is... You Are Magnificent
~
The Tales of Tiernan ~ The Gift of a New Day

Dedication

The book in your hands offers a space to allow one to discover one's truest sense of self. Thoughts to be calmed and to bring forth one's awareness of Divine Beauty Within – for held within is your wisdom to search for your magnificence – there are no mistakes in Divine Creation, and you holding this book and walking upon Mother Earth is *Divine Creation.*

Find your greatest treasures of love for oneself – for you will discover that you are a miracle creating miracles – you are love in its purest form of light.

The book is given with great love, compassion, and kindness, to all that walk upon Mother Earth.

God Bless

Introduction

The writing is conveyed through the gifts of mediumship – through the willingness of the author to share in a grand way the offerings of peace. Peace in one's heart and peace in one's thoughts.

The dialogue is a conversation that will resonate with love held within – for the words speak to one's *Grand Inner Essence* and the words remind us to be gentle with ourselves – to be gentle with our thoughts – the conversation is the unfolding of an awareness of one's truth. Beauty held within to shine light on the darkest corners of life – to guide and to nurture one in the understanding of one's brilliance.

Profound wisdom is held deep within – grand wisdom is shared from the heavens above – your wisdom is to hear your truth of your Inner Essence – to be gentle with all.

God Bless

As the Conversation Unfolds

"Why did you do that? Why were you unkind?"

"*Gentle now*."

"I can't believe how frustrated I am. I can't stand being so angry. Why do people make life miserable?"

"*Gentle now*."

"Why did I bother to try and please another? Why? The person obviously doesn't appreciate what I gave, the time I put in. Why do I let people use me?"

"*Gentle now*."

"I can't stand it. I just can't stand people."

"*Gentle*."

"I can't stand people. People are crazy. I am crazy for listening. I am crazy for trying to fix things. I'm done. I've had it. I am done. I have truly had it. Wait until he gets a piece of my mind. He thinks he can walk on me? Well, I got news for him."

"Gentle... gentle."

"Why do I bother with men? Why do I bother with people? Why do I bother with women? They are all the same, greedy, self-centered, unkind, uncaring. Oh, I've had it. They will hear from me."

"Gentle now. Gentle."

"I need to sit down. I need to calm my mind, calm my thoughts. Damn, I'm mad. I am so angry. It is a good thing for them they aren't here right now... they wouldn't have the nerve to see me after what they have done."

"Gentle... gentle... gentle... gentle... "

"One big breath. Let me sit. Let me sit down to relax and ease my mind.

"Damn, I am so mad. Wait until they hear from me. How dare they treat me the way they did. How dare they, after what I have done for them. How dare they get away with it. I am going to make their life miserable. They don't know who they have crossed. Just wait. I will get them back. Then he will see who wins."

"Gentle, gentle, gentle. Close your eyes, take a breath. Feel your brilliance."

"I hate them. I truly, deeply, hate them."

"Gentle, deep breath. Deep breath and know that you are magnificent."

"I hate them. Just wait. It is exactly like the time years ago when my father did something similar. I hated him. I didn't want to, but he wanted me to hate him, or he would have treated me better."

"Gentle... gentle... deep inhale."

"I'll show them. I will show them. They want to use me, they want to take advantage. I will show them. I will take away what I gave them, then where will they be? I will make them crawl back to me asking, no, begging, to be forgiven. I hate them so much."

"You don't really hate them."

"Okay, a deep breath to ease my mind. I know my thoughts are out of control. I know I shouldn't be this mad. Oh, I am mad. How dare they!"

"Gentle, gentle, gentle."

"How dare they treat me like crap."

"Gentle, gentle, gentle. You know they have a heart."

"Why would they take advantage of me? Why would they, after all I have done? Oh, great. Now I'm going to cry about it."

"Gentle, be soft. Be caring."

"Cry. They aren't going to make me cry. Yes, they are. I hate them for making me cry. I hate them. People that I thought would have my back were the ones that took great advantage of me. Great, now I am crying. I am so mad, so hurt, so beaten. Why does life have to be so hard? Why does life have to be hard for me? Is it only me?"

"Gentle. Life isn't difficult, Sweet One. Life is life, full of love and creation."

"I hate it here. I hate it here. Why am I alive? Oh, I know, for people to take advantage of me, that's why. I came to earth to be used, to be over-looked, to be ignored, unless someone wants something."

"Gentle, Sweet One. It isn't true. You are here for grand reason and great purpose. You must know it from right here."

"I hate crying. I hate being mad. It was a good day. I was having a good day until I found out."

"Gentle."

"I was making improvements. I felt good when I woke up today, and now, I sit in tears and frustration. Why doesn't anyone like me? Why can't I just find peace? Why can I not find love? Why does it have to be so hard?"

"It isn't hard, Sweet One. You are not seeing through the eyes of me."

"Deep breath, stop your crying. You are always such a baby. Wouldn't they love to see you now, crying like a baby. They got what they wanted. Great, the phone is ringing."

"Hello. Yes, I am here. Yes, I got home okay, thank you. Yes, everything is alright. No, I am not upset with you. No, I understand why you did what you did. Yes, I understand. Okay, bye for now.

"Am I okay? They have some nerve to check in on me. They have some nerve to pretend they care. They have such nerve... I hate them. I hate myself. I hate myself for hating them. I am so sad. I can't do this much longer. I can't do life much longer."

"Gentle... gentle... hear my voice. It is a whisper, Sweet One. It is a whisper, Sweet One."

"I should end it all. I should end it all. Who would miss me? Who would care? I hate the way my life is. I hate living in such emotional turmoil. Why is it so difficult to live life? Why are others so awful at times? Why am I so awful to others at times?"

"Gentle, Sweet One. There is no end. You are Eternal Light."

"I live each day thinking and wanting it to be better. Thinking it is going to change, and it doesn't, not since I've been a kid anyway."

"It isn't true. You are blessed beyond your knowing."

"I am not smart. If I was smart, I wouldn't let others take advantage of me. If I was smart, I would tell them all to take a hike. A very long walk off a pier into the depths of water. Well, I probably wouldn't really want that. I just feel so beaten. Why can't it just go smoothly? Why can't I just live life fully, not full of regret and punishment? I must have done something in a past life to be punished in this life."

"*No, it isn't true. You are not punished in this life. Look at you. Look at your brilliance and the miracle that you are. Look within to me.*"

"I thought years ago it would be better. Then I got married to that rascal. He used me. He took advantage of me. He left me. He left me high and dry. High and dry to pick up the pieces. He wanted me to suffer. I hate him too."

"*Sweet One, the marriage ended for it was painful for you. The marriage ended so you would love yourself.*"

"Why would he even marry me? Maybe he was right, I am stupid. I am unattractive. He certainly called me enough names. Why was he so mean and unkind? Why did I let him into my life? Oh, yes, because I am stupid. He was right, he was right all along. I am stupid for thinking someone, even him, would want to spend life with me."

"Love for oneself is the answer, Dear One. Bring forth me."

"I wish I could turn off my thoughts. I wish I could just ease the burdens from my mind. I wish I could stop my anxiety from ruining my days. I wish I could leave. Where would I go? Where would I go?"

"Go within. Find your brilliance. Search for your authentic self. Search for me."

"I want to lay down. I will sleep. I can't sleep. I can never sleep with the worry on my mind. I am so exhausted with life. I am exhausted living with myself. I can't stand myself any longer. I can't stand the world. I can't stand people. I can't stand living like this anymore. I need to nap. I need to rest. I need to find peace in my heart. My heart hurts so much. Why did he leave me? Why was he so mean when he did? Why did he just not find some time to talk with me? He was always so busy, he never paid attention, but then who would? I am unattractive, I am boring, I am unpleasant at times, I'm not good at very much, except trusting people I should never trust."

"*Easy... take care... listen to your words. Hear the lies. It isn't of truth. You are perfection. You must search for your Divine Perfection.*"

"I want to eat. Great, I will eat and gain weight. Can't I have anything in this world that brings happiness without the opposite? Why can't I just have fun? Why does there always have to be a payback, and never something good? Maybe I will have a drink. Yes, a drink. That will ease my mind. I will have a drink. I will lay down and that will ease my mind."

"*Your mind is wanting you to be at peace. Your heart is wanting you to be at peace. Go in search for your greatest peace within. Your mind will calm, when you calm your thoughts of condemnation. Every time you speak unkind words, you take your peaceful heart away.*"

"The room is spinning. I am spinning. Oh, great, they probably will find me dead. Hopefully, someone would find me. Does anyone care? Am I cared for?"

"You are held so lovingly, so beautifully. I have you. I am holding you. You are Divine."

"The room won't stop spinning. Why did I drink so much on an empty stomach? Why did I drink at all? I feel so sick. I feel like dying. No, no, I don't. Yes, I do. No, I don't. If someone was going to find me dead, I want to be wearing something better. Do you hear your thoughts? Who speaks like this? Why am I so hard on myself? Oh, that's right. My husband has gone and married someone else. Someone more pretty. Someone that he actually loves. I don't wish to die. I wouldn't give him the satisfaction. The room is spinning and I feel awful, and he is probably having a great day. He is probably romancing his new romance of new marriage. It's all BS. It is rotten. My life is rotten."

"You are magnificent. Hear my whisper. You are magnificent."

"What time is it? Oh, God, what time is it? How long have I been asleep? The room stopped spinning, thankfully. Why do I drink the way I do? I don't like who I have become. I don't like that I have lived up to the ones that called me names. My husband said that I wouldn't give up drinking, and I did for a while, but I didn't know that he would leave when he did. I didn't know he had met someone else. I didn't know how cruel life could be. How cruel life is for me. I need a drink. I drink to drown. I drink to drown."

"Gentle, hear my words. Hear my whisper. I love you."

"Ah, I can't move. Wouldn't he like to see this. He would think that I am longing for him, that I can't live without him. I will show him. I will show him. He showed me. Let's face it, he got the winning end of the stick. He won the prize, he won the new wife, he won leaving me to rot. He won."

"Sweet One, it isn't about winning. Sweet One, find love within, find your gift of compassion."

"I bet he is still on his honeymoon. He wanted me to drink. He led me to drink. I drink because of the man he was... the man he is. Oh, I am sure, his new honey will be drinking in no time, that, or she drinks now. Perhaps, they deserve each other. I need that drink. I need many drinks."

"*Love for oneself.*"

"The walk to the cabinet always feels longer than it should. At least I don't keep the bottles beside my bed. He would love to see that. Me, drunk, over him. Me, passed out with a broken heart while he makes love to his bride.

"I don't need ice. In fact, I don't need a glass. Have some class, you need a glass. When was the last time I did the dishes?"

"*Forgiveness for yourself, Sweet One.*"

"Look at the pile of dishes. Oh, he would love to see this. All the times I heard, 'Clean this place up, you live like a pig.' A pig? He called me a pig. He called me a pig while he was having an affair. So I don't do the dishes as often as I should, so what!"

"*Find your way by hearing my voice. Hear the whisper. I am you.*"

"Okay, where is that glass? Of course, in the sink with the rest. Out of the bottle it is, at least until I can clean up."

"*Water, Sweet One, drink water.*"

"Damn my heart hurts. My head hurts. Why

do I have a mirror in the kitchen? Oh, yes, to remind me of why he left. Why can't I open this bottle? Why can't I get my life together? I am such a mess. Who is looking back at me? I hate this mirror. I hate looking at me. I hate myself and I hate my life. I want, I want, I want to be me again."

"You are not lost, listen to my whisper. You are right here with me, safe. I am holding you in safety."

"What have you done to yourself? Look at your hair. Look at your wrinkles. I will never meet anyone. I don't want to meet anyone... probably, just like the others. They will use me, they will take advantage, and pretend, yes, pretend, they love me, and then they will leave me. Just like my family. Just like my mom. That's not fair, my mom passed. I am sure she didn't want to leave me. Stop crying. Where is that bottle opener? I have wine. I have wine. Wine is good out of the bottle. Here it is. Okay, deep breath, find strength to open the wine bottle."

"Your strength is within. Go within to seek your beauty and brilliance. Hear my voice,

hear me as I am you."

"How much wine can I drink? The bottle is almost empty, just like my heart. I give up. I want to give up. Oh, the phone is ringing again. Can't they all just leave me alone? It will go to the answering machine."

"Take a deep breath and hear your heart call forth the whisper of the Universe."

"They didn't leave a message. They don't care. Telemarketers don't even want to hear my voice."

"Hear your Inner Voice, Sweet One."

"Great, they are calling back. Hello. Hello. Helloo. They hung up. Go to hell."

"There is no hell. The hell is you beating upon yourself."

"Who left the chair in the middle of the room? I hate stubbing my toe. Why is the chair here? I am the only one here. Why do I move furniture around when I drink? Why do I drink? Why do I even care that I drink? Some people do much worse. I should have spent his money. I was so fair. I should have taken every dime. I was deserving after what he has caused. I want to die.

"The phone again. Come on. You better be on the other end. Hello. Yes, I am home. Yes, I am okay. Why wouldn't I be okay? Yes, I know, I haven't turned on the lights. Yes, thank you for checking in on me. I will turn on my outdoor lights, thank you. I know you get concerned, but I am fine. Thank you, have a good evening. Please say hello to your wife for me. Goodbye.

"The nerve, checking in on me. Bloody nosey neighbours. They would know if I died. They would be here to make sure my outside light was on. Oh... why am I so angry and mean? They are so kind to check in on me, and I am miserable. They probably feel sorry for me. Yes, sorry that my husband left with a younger girl. I won't call her a lady. I'm not a lady. Look at me. Drunk on a Wednesday evening. Drunk once again. That's why he left. I am a drunk, a no good fool of a woman."

"*Easy... gentle... quiet. Quiet your mind to hear me guide you. Hear your loving-self guide you to your magnificence.*"

"What time is it? Ten. Ten o'clock and I can't find my way to my bed. I am so exhausted. Drunk and exhausted. At least my outdoor light is on to take care of the necessary things. I find that funny. I used to have humour. What happened to my laughter? What happened to me singing? I guess the days of happiness are over. I have become miserable in my existence. I got to go to bed, another early morning for me to exist in my emptiness."

"Sleep, Sweet One. Rest your mind, rest your body, rest your soul. We are One, Sweet One, we are One."

"I hate the alarm clock. I hate waking up. I hate my days. I hate my hangovers. I hate myself. What am I going to wear today? How am I going to make it through the day once again? Come on, get your lazy body out of bed. Ugh... I can't move. Perhaps I will call in sick. Yes, I will tell them I cannot go in today. Oh, I did that last week. Come on, into the shower. I hate my day starting like this. Another mirror to remind me of my aging body. I am getting rid of all the mirrors. They haunt me, they remind me of what I once was, and what I have become."

"Careful, be gentle with your words. You are magnificent. See your body temple as a temple. See you as you truly are... magnificent."

"Why did I leave the shampoo bottle empty in the shower? Don't you do anything right? Don't you know how to take care of yourself? Loser. Can't even replace the empty bottle. I replace empty wine bottles with no problem. Oh, that reminds me, I better stop at the liquor store. Where do I spend my money? On booze. Why do I spend my money on booze? To feel better than this. I like to drink. I do feel better. Just thinking about feeling better, makes me feel better."

"Think of your laughter, Sweet One. Think of your joy. Think of your greatness. Find forgiveness, find compassion for oneself."

"Is there not a clean towel? When was the last time I did laundry? I better get this place cleaned up or they will come after me. Who will come after me? Nobody cares if my house is a mess, or not. Nobody visits, nobody cares how I live. Hell, I don't care how I live.

"Is today the day I am to be at work early for

that meeting? What day is it? Damn, I have forgotten about the stupid meeting. I hate the meetings, everyone is happy and full of life. I sit and look around at the others knowing they are happy because they didn't have someone leave them for another."

"You are whole, you are Divine Creation. Listen to your Divine Creation within."

"I better wear something better today. When did I do laundry? I'm going to have to call in sick. No, no, I can't. I have to be there. I have to be there. I used to love my job. I was good at my job. Now, well now, I only exist at life. Please tell me I have gas in the car. Did I stop for gas yesterday? I hate living. So much to do. So much to do. I can't eat breakfast. I don't have time for breakfast. Another morning with coffee. I will stop on my way for coffee. They might have donuts at the meeting."

"Drink water, Sweet One. Nourish your body temple."

"I feel so sad, so drained. I miss my youth. I miss my prettiness. I miss me so much.

"Where are my keys? Shoot, where did I leave

my keys? I hate this day! I hate mornings! I hate myself for messing up my life! I messed up my life. No, he messed up my life, he and his new pretty wife. They messed up everything. I am so tired. Don't cry, don't cry. Put some make-up on. Get your mascara on so you don't cry. God, I can't look in the mirror. Okay... how do I make this face look better? Look at the bags under my eyes. He would love to see this. He would love to see my demise of me, of life."

"*Listen to me, your Inner Essence of you. Listen to my whisper of only love for you. You are Inner Beauty. There are no mistakes in Creation. There are no mistakes in Creation*."

"Why do I bother? I can't get anything right. I've messed up my make-up, my hair is a mess. What did you think it would look like without shampoo, stupid? Okay, I will wear my hair in a ponytail. He hated when I wore my hair in a ponytail. Mom always liked my hair down, but then again, I was a kid with shampoo! One, two, three... count to three. Count to three, deep breath."

"*Sweet One, take a deep breath for*

nourishment. A deep breath to ease your thoughts. Stop condemning yourself. Only kind words, Sweet One, only kind words."

"I wish I could be a kid again. Boy, I would do it over. I would be smart. I would have paid more attention about people and their lies. I trusted everyone, and now, I trust no one. No one is worth trusting. Who can I trust? Who can I trust to speak the truth? He didn't speak the truth. He lied every chance, covering up his honey. Why did he leave me for someone else? Why couldn't he have just left without having my replacement? Why didn't I know sooner? I am such a doorknob. I saw the signs, I didn't want to look. I didn't want the truth. I guess I lied to myself. I am just like everyone else, a liar. A no good liar. People lie to me because I lie to myself."

"*See the truth in your beauty.*"

"I can't stand this mirror. I know some mirrors make you look awful. This mirror makes me look awful. It's the lighting. I hate bright lights. I hate seeing my old body. I'm not old. I just feel old. He made me old. He feels young. He has someone younger that makes him feel young. God, I wish I would have washed my hair. I remember when I used to take care of my hair and make-up. I had nice nails and nice clothes. I had a much better life. I had shoes. Remember the shoes I wore. I loved my heels, and now, I wear old shoes without heels. I feel awful. I hate hangovers. I hate hangovers during the week. Why did I drink so much? Why do I drink so much?"

"*Kindness, compassion, love. Kindness, compassion, love towards yourself. Be gentle with yourself.*"

"Okay, I am ready... Not really. Can I have a drink? I can put it in my coffee. No, no, don't be foolish. You're foolish enough as it is. You need to get out of this house on time. You need to be at the stupid meeting. You need to replace the shampoo bottle."

"*Quiet your mind. Quiet your mind.*"

"Why does the drive have to be so hard? Stupid drivers. Everyone should be off the road. They all drive like maniacs. I should start taking the bus... this way, I could drink. No, I would lose my job for sure."

"Quiet your mind. Speak gently."

"I hope I find parking. I always wanted my own parking space. Had I got the raise and the transfer, I would have my own parking spot... probably with my name on it. But, no, I was stupid and stayed in this city because he wanted to stay here. Yes, he wanted to stay to be with his honey. I hate him. He would love that I don't have my own parking spot. I could have been so much more without him."

"You are magnificent."

"Just in time for the stupidness of co-workers. Why didn't I open my own business? I could have, but I didn't think I had what it took. I didn't have money. He spent the money. I spent the money. I should have opened my business, then I would be proud of something."

"Gentle. You are everything."

"There is the boss. She has her own spot. Look at her smiling. She must wonder why I don't have a better car. She probably thinks that I am a loser."

"You are magnificent."

"In I go. Another day, another dollar, so they say. I can't wait to get out of here. I can't wait to leave this place. Maybe I should change cities. I wouldn't be here with them."

"Go within to find your Inner Essence. Go within, in your search for your greatness."

"Oh, God, I have spilled my coffee on my blouse. I am such a loser. Do I have time to wash it out? No, I will be late. I will just have to announce that I can't drink my morning coffee without acting like a child."

"Gentle with yourself. Gentle."

"Look at all these happy faces. Why do I put on a fake smile? Maybe, just maybe, they are fake. What if each person around this boardroom table was feeling just like me, empty, and really not wanting to be here? I guess we all lie, we lie with our expressions on our face, for I truly feel like tears."

"Find your Inner Strength."

"What?! What! The place is going to close? What? We are losing our jobs? Are you kidding me? Are you kidding me? You asked for this meeting to ruin our lives. Why is the boss smiling? Why am I sitting here listening to the BS of why they are closing? They are closing! I can't believe it! Great, I have lost my job, the one thing I have. It is lost too. Nobody is smiling now... Am I to feel sorry for these people? They have spouses, they probably have money. I lost my job. I have nothing left. There is nothing more for me here. Why am I even alive?"

"Gentle, gentle. Create your future by hearing my whisper. You are not alone."

"I can't believe this garbage they are dishing out. Wow, we get to stay another two weeks, this is BS... beyond BS. Who do they think they are? Using us, using me to get something, and now, they are closing the place. I can't believe this is happening to me. Why didn't I take that other job away from this stupid place? Why didn't I open my business? Why didn't I just know to do something better than this?"

"Easy. Gentle. You are safe. I will guide you. You are Divine Creation of Divine Creation. You are whole."

"I'm out of here. Do I stay until the end of the

meeting? What's the point? Oh, God, they are serving donuts. Nothing like rubbing it in our faces. Here, have a donut, even though we just messed up your life. Here, stuff your face with fattening donuts. It may be your last meal for there are no paycheques. Such BS. I want to cry so badly. I wish I could talk to my mom."

"*Your mom is with you. She is holding you. Your mom is Divine Creation holding you in your own Light of Grace.*"

"I can't cry. Why does everyone look so calm? Why can't they see what is happening? My life is over as I know it and everyone is having a bloody donut."

"*Easy...*"

"Oh, we get to take the day off with pay. Isn't that nice. Feed us more crap. And this is to make me feel better? The boss is still smiling. She probably got a transfer. She probably got my transfer. I want to go home. I do need a drink. I don't care what bloody time it is. I need a drink. What am I going to do? What am I going to do?"

"*Follow your heart. Hear the whisper of love*

to guide you. You are magnificent. You will thrive in beauty."

"Maybe, I will take a donut for the road. It is such BS. Look at everyone shaking hands like a great business deal has been awarded. We lost our jobs. Can anyone see that? They are all smiling, and understanding, kissing up to the boss. Probably ready to hand in their résumé for the new location. Sucking up to the boss even after they lose their job. Jerks."

"*Easy. Easy. Condemning others only hurts yourself.*"

"I am so shaky. How am I going to drive home? Just get in your car. Get in your car. Smile as you leave the room. Be cordial and smile like the rest of the fake people. Everything is so fake. Smiles are so fake."

"*Easy. You have reason to celebrate.*"

"I hate this place. I hate my life, and now I really hate it. I hate God for this. I hate being here. I have to get to my car before I cry, before I breakdown. I can't have these losers see me cry."

"*Inner strength, Sweet One. Inner strength.*"

"Okay, pull yourself together. Pull yourself together before heading into the liquor store. Easy driving, almost there. I can't believe I lost my job today. I can't believe I lost my life. Where did it go? Where did I go? What happened? Why am I being punished? I am a good person, a really good person, and this BS keeps happening. Why has my life turned so bad? What did I do to deserve this life of punishment?"

"You are the creator of your next step. Follow my lead. Follow your Inner Guidance. Follow your heart and wisdom. You are the creator of your next step."

"Okay, two bottles in the cart. No, three bottles... I have all day. Should I take four? Perhaps I should really wallow in my misery."

"Celebrate who you are, Sweet One. Celebrate your brilliance."

"Yes, sir, four bottles today. I am having company for supper. A dinner party, and thankfully we all like the same thing. Yes, sir, you have a wonderful day.

"A wonderful day... dinner company. You lie.

You lie all the time and you expect people to tell you the truth. Loser. I have become a loser that pretends to have a good life. Nobody would be coming for a dinner party. I used to love entertaining. I used to love many things. I miss my dog. I miss my life. Don't cry. Don't cry. I miss you, mom."

"Your mom is you in Eternal Light. Listen to the love in your heart. Listen to your whisper of love speak to you. It is a whisper, Sweet One. Calm your mind. Listen."

"Okay, almost home, almost home. How much longer can I do this? Where am I going to work? How am I going to pay for everything? How am I going to live now? This house is so empty. I should move. Perhaps, I should sell my house. That will get me through until I find a job. The house is empty. My heart is empty. Thank God, my wine glass is full. Time to sit. Time to ease my mind. Time to have a good cry."

"Gentle with yourself, gentle with yourself. Nourish and heal with your tears. You are Divine Perfection."

"Okay, where are the tissues? Where are the

tissues? I'm using the back of my sleeve like I did when I was five. I wish I was five. I wish my mom was still here to look after me. Everyone has left me. I am all alone. Why am I all alone?"

"*You are not alone, Sweet One. Hear the gentle whisper of loving guidance. Hear me, I am you. I am Divine Creation. Hear me, hear my whisper.*"

"There must be something better. There must be something better for me. It's best I don't have a dog, I can't keep care of myself."

"*Care for yourself. You can. Find the love held within. Find you.*"

"What am I going to eat for lunch? What's in the fridge? I haven't done groceries. Look at this kitchen. Look at this mess. I never lived like this before. If my husband was still here, he would leave for sure. He called me a pig, look at me, I do live like a pig. I like pigs, they are cute. Pigs get a bad rap."

"*Easy. Find your way by stillness.*"

"Okay, not much to eat, but lots to drink. Cheers."

"*Water, drink water.*"

"Why is this chair in the middle of the room? Look at this place, it is a pigsty. I do live like a pig. Stop your crying. You're such a baby, a loser, a pig loser. Okay, I am not a loser. Yes, yes, I am. Look around, look at myself."

"*Look deep within. Look Through the Eyes of Me.*"

"I can't stand all these mirrors. I can't stand looking at myself anymore. Who have I become? Who am I?"

"*You are The Great I Am.*"

"Look at my wrinkles. Dry your tears. Stop blubbering like a baby. Dry your tears. Wipe your mascara off your face. I hate the way I look. Why is the phone ringing again?

"Pull yourself together. Hello. Yes, I am home. Yes, I have received bad news today. Yes, my office is closing. Is it on the news already? Yes, I will be fine. I will be fine. Thank you for checking in, and I will make sure to have my lights on this evening for you. Thank you for calling. Bye for now."

"Calm your mind, calm your thoughts."

"I hate feeling helpless. I hate this life. I hate my life. Why is all this horrible stuff happening to me? I haven't recovered from my divorce. I haven't recovered from losing my mom. I haven't recovered from losing... me. Stop crying. Crying won't change a thing. Put on your big girl pants and stop your crying. Have another drink. I feel awful."

"Stop beating upon yourself. You are perfection."

"Okay, no food in the house. I can't drive now with all that I drank. I have no one to call for help. I hate this life. Is that the doorbell? Oh, God, I look awful. I can't open the door now. They keep knocking. Who is it? Wipe your tears and mascara. Open the door."

"Be gentle and know you are not alone."

"Hello. Oh, it is you. Please, please forgive my appearance. You know I am having a rather difficult day. It was such a shock to lose my job. Your wife sent me lunch? Why? Thank you for thinking of me. I do love homemade soup, thank you. There is plenty, enough to last me for a few meals. You are lucky to have such a beautiful wife. Please, please thank her, and thank you for thinking of me. You have been very kind, thank you. Bye for now."

"Gentle with yourself."

"They gave me food when they didn't know I didn't have anything to eat. How did they know that I needed help when I did? They lovingly gave to me the one thing that I did need in this moment. Not just food, but the knowing that someone... cares."

"Nourish your body, Sweet One. It is a gift from the heavens above."

"Can I eat after all that I have drank? I wonder if he could smell the booze. They must know I am a loser. Stop crying. Stop crying. When you drink too much you cry like a baby. Stop it."

"Gentle. Stop beating upon yourself. You are deeply loved."

"My head is spinning. I can't think. I can't concentrate. My life is a mess. My life doesn't ever get better. Why would my life not get better? Stop crying, baby. You are such a baby. Who is going to take you seriously? My head hurts. I drank too much. I've cried too much, and I don't want to leave my bed. Not today, not today."

"Gentle, make time for nourishment. Take time to nourish oneself."

"What time is it? How long have I slept? The whole day? The whole day gone... thank God. Thank God, I didn't have to deal with anyone today. No thoughts, no pain, no anger. I slept off the drinks, and thankfully, I rested."

"Easy. Your body needs water. Your body is asking for nourishment. Your mind is asking for nourishment. Your heart is wanting to heal your pain and suffering. Gentle, Sweet One. Gentle with yourself."

"Oh, my head. It feels as big as this room. I can't move. What time is it? It's close to supper. I have no food and I certainly can't drive. Oh, wait, the neighbour brought soup. I have soup. I have soup. Stop crying. Stop your damn crying."

"Gentle, nourish your body for healing. Ease

your thoughts for healing. Stop beating upon yourself for healing."

"I can't get up. I'll wait. I will wait here. I will wait. Perhaps, I will just die here. Maybe I'm better off. Maybe nobody would care. Maybe, just maybe, it would be peaceful."

"Ease your mind. Your thoughts will ease. Hear my whisper. Understand you are more than life experience. Understand, you are Divine Creation."

"I wish things were better. I remember when they were so much better. I had my husband, my beautiful dog, the house was clean, I was happy. I remember how good life was before it all fell apart. I wish mom was here. I wish mom was here."

"Your mom is holding you. Your mom is in deep care for you. Feel your heart. Hear the whisper of your own heart. You will find love."

"Mom, if you can hear me... Mom, if you can hear me, I need you. I need help here. I need you, mom. Please... please, mom, I need you."

"Hear your heart, Sweet One. Hear your heart."

"Mom, I messed up. Mom, I messed up my life. I hate it here. I wish I was with you. Mom, just to hear your voice. You'd be telling me to get up, to get up and start with a step."

"*Listen, listen carefully.*"

"Mom, please... please, mom, I need you. I need something from the heavens, from God. Please can anyone hear me?"

"*You are being held. Your words are heard without the sound of your voice. Listen. Listen for your wisdom in your answers. Listen for the wisdom that your mom is holding for you.*"

"Mom? Can anyone hear me? Can anyone hear me? Please, my head hurts, my heart is broken, I've messed up my life. Everyone has left me."

"*Quiet your mind, Sweet Child, and hear your own Inner Wisdom speak with you. To guide you, to nurture you, to love you beyond any love that you know.*"

"Mom, I am sorry I messed things up. I always wanted you to be proud of me. Mom, I am sorry. You wouldn't find your nights holding a bottle in your hand. Mom, I need to ease my pain and my sorrow. I have failed you."

"You haven't failed, Sweet One, you are experiencing life."

"Oh, stop crying. I wish I could just stop crying. What happened to me? When did I lose myself?"

"You are not lost. You are not lost."

"Please, mom, I need you to show me a sign. Anything, mom. Anything that would let me know that you still are here with me, that you haven't left me to rot here... alone."

"Gentle, you are flourishing. You are finding a way to find your greatest self. You have chosen a pathway to find who you truly are underneath layers of human experience."

"Mom... can you hear me? I can't stop crying. I can't go on living like this. My head hurts, my heart is in so much pain, and I am not even sure why."

"Life experience has led you to discover the greatest you."

"Mom... where did I go wrong? Was it the

marriage? Was it the divorce? Was it not opening up my business when I had the chance?"

"*You have another chance. You have made room in your life to have your desires.*"

"Mom, if you could say something, anything, what would you say? I know you would only love me like a mother should. I bet you would tell me to get up, to put on some lipstick and to start cleaning this pig pen."

"*Gentle, gentle, gentle.*"

"Mom, is there a way I can hear you?"

"*Gentle, quiet your mind. Quiet your thoughts.*"

"Is that a knock at the door? Who is at the door at this time?

"My outside light isn't turned on. I have slept too long. I can't move. Just go away. Leave me to just die here. I hate it here. I want to see my mom."

"*Easy, gentle, hear your heart whisper the love you are holding.*"

"What is that knocking? What is that knocking? I have to get up. Please make the world go away. Make the world go away."

"*Your world is open to the grandest love for oneself.*"

"I don't see anyone. I'll turn on the outdoor light. Perhaps, it was just the neighbour."

"*Easy... drink water.*"

"I don't see anything. Is there a note at the door? No note. Maybe it was my imagination. Maybe, just maybe, I heard the knocking only in my head. I have to stop drinking. I drink too much. I hate this mirror! Why do I have so many mirrors?! I hate seeing myself like this. I am a wreck and nobody cares. Hell, I don't even care. Where is my glass?"

"*Easy, nourish yourself.*"

"Why don't I care? When did I stop caring? When did I stop caring for myself? I don't know. Life has handed me a bad hand. I don't get it. I am a good person. I was raised by good people. I miss my grandmother. She would have an answer for me. She would tell me to get on with life, that drowning my sorrows wasn't going to help. Grandmothers know best. This drinking isn't helping. What is in the fridge?"

"Gentle, Sweet One. Listen to your guidance. Listen to the love you hold within."

"I haven't done groceries for so long. What day is it? Perhaps I'll go on the weekend. Perhaps, I will find my way. Way to what, more struggle, more upset and discouragement? Every day is the same. I struggle, I drink, I sleep it off. I need to get my life in order. I need to."

"Sweet Child, listen to your heart. Find the stillness in the moment to listen to your heart."

"I have to sit down. I don't know what happened to me. Was it after mom died that I truly lost my way? I miss you, mom. I miss you. What I would give to hear your voice once again. To eat ice cream with you once again. Mom... I'm in trouble here. I am not functioning like a normal adult should. I feel like a child that doesn't know where to go. I am lost. I feel like a child, lost without knowing where to go. Mom, please. God, please. Someone, please help me find my way.

"There is that knock. Who is it? Probably some brat on the street. I don't want to get up to answer the door. Are they still there? Stupid kids in the neighbourhood. Oh, stop. Listen to yourself. You love kids, you are just mad that you didn't have any. Thank goodness, I never had children, I can't look after myself. Maybe life would have been better with someone to love. Someone that loved me back. I should have had children when I had the chance. It takes two, and the other now married with his young bride, probably planning a family.

"What is the knocking? I'm getting up, and someone better be standing at the door to deal with me.

"I can't see anyone, even with the outside light on.

"There it is again. It's not from the front door. What is that knocking? Am I losing my mind? Probably, that's all I need, to lose my mind. Well, I've lost everything else, why not my mind?"

"*Gentle, easy, be open to receive your own inner guidance and nurturing. You are held in the wholeness of life itself.*"

"I am going to turn on every light in this house. Perhaps, they will think that I am not alone. I know I am alone, but nobody needs to know that, especially the ones playing around outside.

"Where is that knocking coming from? Stop it."

"*Listen to your heart. Find the stillness in the wholeness of your heart.*"

"I don't understand life. I don't understand hard times. I don't understand why I can't get my life to work. Why can't I get my life to work? I've lost my job. I live alone while my ex-husband sleeps with his new bride. My mom died, unexpectedly. I am lost. Why does life have to be like this? Why do I have a constant struggle? Why, why, why, why, why?"

"*Easy, Sweet Child, for you are heard in the heavens. Listen to the gentle whisper of your heart.*"

"Well, the knocking has stopped. I wonder who is around the house at this time of night? Probably kids playing jokes on people. Great,

I have become the miserable old lady on the street that the kids laugh at and torment. Why does it have to be this hard? Can anyone hear me? Does anyone care? I don't care. You know, if you can hear me and you don't answer, why should I believe in anything but this crappy life? I thought God hears everything. I thought that my prayers would be answered. Look what I have, sweet nothing at all. God doesn't hear my words. God doesn't answer a prayer. I'm going to bed."

"*You are Divine. Your words are always heard and answers are always present. Listen carefully for the guidance.*"

"When was the last time I changed the sheets on my bed? When was the last time I changed anything? I hate my life. I can't stand myself anymore. I don't want to be here. Please, please, I am asking to know that I am not alone. I am asking you, God, to give me a sign. Please, just a sign. Please, mom, are you there? Don't send kids to knock on the door. I need to know. I need to know someone, anyone, cares about me."

"*Listen, Sweet Child. Listen to your heart in*

the stillness of silence. You must be still to hear the whisper."

"God, are you there? Mom, are you there? Great, just silence and the sound of the clock ticking, letting me know that I am getting older as time goes on. Tick-tock, tick-tock, that is the only thing I will hear. The sound of time passing without anything changing."

"Listen to your heart's whisper."

"There is that knocking again. I have had it. Now I am really mad. You better be there when I open the door, stupid kid. You better run before I call the police and tell your parents. Stupid kids, don't they know that people are suffering?"

"You must be still. Be still."

"One, two, three. I am opening this door. You better run! What are you doing? I am not opening the door. What if it is a stranger to rob me? Go away!"

"Quiet. Quiet your mind."

"I said go away. Leave me alone. I will call the police!"

"Quiet your mind."

"Why am I yelling? I can't see anything outside. They must have run away. It probably is the neighbour's brats having nothing better to do than to pick on the crazy lady down the street.

"I am crazy. I have lost my mind. God, can you hear me? Mom! Can you hear me? Why am I yelling? They aren't going to answer. Mom! Mom! God! Mom! God! God! Where are you when you are needed?"

"Quiet. Be still and know that you are One."

"Is that the knocking? Stop knocking, you brats! Stop knocking!

"Can't a girl have any peace? Where is God anyway? This praying is nonsense. Who listens? Nobody.

"I am going back to bed. Perhaps, I won't wake up. If there is a God, he should take me now. I hate my life. Give my life to someone who really cares. Give my life to someone who wants to live. God, where are you now?"

"You are Eternal Light and Divine Grace."

"God, if you can hear me, I am asking... No... right now I am pleading for a sign. Pleading to know that I exist. Pleading to know that I am going to be okay. Please, God, please. Please send me something, anything, before I don't believe at all."

"Listen to your heart, Sweet One. Divine, whispers to your heart."

"God, please. Please."

"Listen. Quiet. Ease your mind."

"I don't see you. I don't hear you. I don't even feel you. Are you real? Do you exist? Is there really a God?"

"Listen. Listen. It is in the stillness."

"Why am I alone? Why did I lose everything? Why was I not smarter, or stronger? Why do I suffer so? Why do I drink so much? I miss my mom. I miss myself. God, are you there?"

"Gentle... gentle... gentle... "

"Okay. Deep breath. Deep breath. One, two, three... Deep breath. Deep breath. My heart is racing. Deep breath. Deep breath. My heart is broken. Deep breath. Inhale, exhale. Deep breath. I can't breathe. I can't breathe. My stomach is turning. My head is spinning. God, please. I am now begging. God, please let me know that I am going to be okay. I know I said I wanted to die, but I don't. I want to live without heartache and loss. I want to live, but not like this. I don't wish to live like this anymore."

"Quiet. Be still. Be still and know that you are held in Loving Arms of Grace."

"Deep breath. Deep breath. Deep breath. That feels better. I can hear my heart pound in my chest. Please, I need you now. Somebody, please. Deep breath. Deep breath. Don't stop breathing. Deep breath. My heart is so loud. My heart feels like it is going to explode. Deep breath. Deep breath. God, please don't answer my prayer of me wanting to die. Please, God, don't answer that prayer. I hurt all over. I hurt, and I just wanted life to stop hurting. But I want to live. God, please give me a sign you know I want to live.

"Deep breath. Deep breath. Deep breath. Calm your mind. Calm your heart. Calm. Deep breath. Deep breath. Mom, are you there?

Mom, hold my hand. Mom, please hold my hand. I'm having trouble breathing mom. Please hold my hand. Deep breath. Deep breath. Deep breath. Okay, relax. Relax. Relax. Deep breath. Deep breath. Relax. Relax. Relax. Relax. Relax. Deep breath. Relax. Relax."

"*Ease your thoughts. Release the pain. Release and hear your Inner Essence guide you.*"

"Where did I go wrong? I miss my childhood. Think of something good. Deep breath. Deep breath. Think happy thoughts. Deep breath. I miss my childhood. I miss my friends. I miss the cat I had. I loved that cat. Why did my father give the cat away? I hated him for giving the cat away. It was my cat, not his. I loved that cat. Did I go wrong there? Did I go wrong pretending that it was okay and that I really didn't love her. I let him give her away. I thought I would be strong. I didn't want to be attached. I hated him so, and then I had to live with that. How can anyone hate their father? He gave away the one thing that was close to me."

"Quiet your mind. Ease your thoughts."

"Deep breath. Deep breath. Think of something good, like cookies and milk. I am hungry. When did I eat last? Deep breath. I know when I drank last. I have to stop drinking. I just have to get my life together. Deep breath. One... breathe. Two... breathe. Three... breathe. Deep breath. Think of something really good. My wedding day. It was so perfect. The weather was so beautiful. I was beautiful. Where did my beauty go? Where did I go? Deep breath. Breathe. Just breathe slowly. I had the prettiest gown. My mom... Mom, I need you. I need you now. Deep breath. Deep breath. Easy. Go easy. It was so wonderful that mom helped me make and design my gown. We worked so hard to make it so perfect... and it was perfect. It was perfect. I miss you, mom. Thank you for everything."

"Quiet your mind. Know that you are held in loving arms."

"Mom, why did you have to leave me? Can I forgive you? Why did my husband leave? Can I forgive him? And dad, well he left when I was so little. You were happy when he left. You were relieved that he left. Why can't I be just like you? Why can't I be happy my husband left me? Deep breath. Just breathe."

"*Easy. Your life experience has created a space for you to find your Inner Love. Love for yourself.*"

"Mom, remember the day he packed up and left? You came home to a note. At least he was man enough to leave a note. My husband didn't. I had to find a love letter from his lover. Not a note saying goodbye. Mom, do you remember that day? You said you were finally a free woman. Mom, why can't I be like you? Why can't I see the world like you saw it?"

"*See the world through Divine. See the world Through the Eyes of Divine. You are One.*"

"Mom, remember you took me out to the local diner to have ice cream? I don't think I ever saw you look more attractive, more radiant, than the day my father left you. Why, mom, why can't I be like you?"

"*See your world Through the Eyes of Source.*"

"Mom, he really mistreated you. I never had

such a wonderful ice cream treat in all my life than that day. Mom, can we go for ice cream? Is there ice cream in heaven, mom?

"You were so young, too. Why didn't you just panic that you had me to raise on your own? Mom, I couldn't take care of the dog. You were strong. I am not. Why mom, why didn't you give me more of things like you? We were always so opposite. We fought so much as I got older. We just didn't see the world the same, and now, I wish I could be just like you. Maybe, I thought it was your fault dad left. Is that when it went wrong for me?"

"Easy. Find comfort with your breath."

"Deep breath. Deep breath. That feels better. My tears have stopped anyway. My heart feels crushed. I am so angry. I am so hurt. I am so frustrated. I am so beaten. I am so frail. I am so overwhelmed. I am so stupid."

"Easy, Sweet Child. Only kindness towards oneself."

"The house is so quiet. Just me and the ticking of the clocks. How can I stop time? How can I go back in time to fix what was so broken? I am so broken. How do I fix me? When do I fix me?"

"Easy. Quiet. Listen to your heart speak gently to you."

"Time goes so fast, the years are just slipping away. What have I done with my life? What have I done? Maybe I should get another dog. No... I can't look after myself. I didn't want the dog to leave. I feel so empty and so helpless. I feel so helpless. Mom, are you there? Please, mom, I need you now. I really want to know that I am not alone. It's so quiet here, mom. I miss your voice. I miss your footsteps. What a funny thing to miss. You always wore your heels. It was your trademark. I could hear you miles away. Gosh, why am I not like you? Why do I wear shoes that are unattractive? I gave up on myself, mom. I gave up looking after myself. That's why he left. I gave up looking after myself."

"Sweet Child, you are here for grand reason and great purpose. You are here to shine your loving light. You must go in search for your loving light to share."

"I hated shopping with you, mom. You were

always so happy to go. You had a great figure. I wish I was more like you. I wish I was thin and fit like you were. You really looked after yourself, mom. Who would have ever thought that you would die so young?"

"There is no death, Sweet One. There is only a transition into the grandest self."

"Why do people have to die? Why do people have to leave? Why do people stay? Why do people stay when life isn't feeling very good? If I was honest with myself, I know I was staying in a marriage that wasn't a happy marriage. I stayed to fix it, but maybe it couldn't be fixed. Maybe, we were meant to part. Maybe, my mom died when she was to die. Who makes the rules? Who chooses? Do we have a choice? Do we have any choices?"

"Each moment is a choice, Sweet One. Each moment is a choice to choose."

"Did I have choices? Did I want choices? Maybe, just maybe, I wanted all things to look good. I wanted people to think I had it all together. That my life was together. A husband, a nice home, perhaps going to start a family. I had a good job, he has a good job, we were the epitome of success, and inside, inside our hearts, inside our home, we were truly empty. Who decides that? Who decides to feel empty when there is so much that should feel full? I bet he feels full now. I bet he is happy with his young bride. I bet they will have children. It is too late for me... Maybe I will get another dog. I can't look after the houseplants right now. I can't look after myself right now. I am such an idiot, such a failure. Why did I stay in a marriage that should have ended long before it did? Why did I wait until he left me? If I left first, if I left him, perhaps, just maybe, I would feel like something. Maybe I would have had the honey on the side. I just couldn't do it. Tied to the wedding vows, tied to wanting something fixable. I should have left him. I should have. What would life look like now? Would I be drunk in bed wanting my life to end or to get better?"

"Listen. Be gentle. You are here for grand reason and great purpose. You are here. You are here. Choose to feel here."

"What would I have done had I left first? I would have opened my florist shop. Mom wanted me to. Mom knew I could do it. I was scared of failing. I knew I was failing at the marriage, at being a wife. That I understood. I guess, I felt like a failure before I even started. I am sorry, mom, for not listening to you. I am sorry. Look at me now because I didn't listen to you."

"*Listen to your Inner Essence of all that you are. Listen to the gentle nudge that is sharing with you that you are of grand purpose. There are no mistakes in Creation. Listen to your heart.*"

"Okay, breathe. Just breathe. One deep breath. One deep breath. One deep breath. One deep breath. One deep breath."

"*Listen to the whisper.*"

"Oh my, what time is it? The sun is shining. What day is it? Where am I? Oh, in bed. My bed. I woke up. I am awake. I am here. I didn't die in my sleep. I woke to this new day. I woke to the sun shining. My head hurts so much. How much did I drink last night? How much did I drink? I am a fool. Stop crying. Stop crying. Pull yourself together. Stop your damn crying. You are such a baby. Breathe.

Just breathe. I am here. I am safe. I hurt all over. God, do I thank you for keeping me here? I miss my mom. I don't like my life here, God. How do I change it? You gave me another day. How do I change?"

"*Listen. Listen to your Divine held within. Listen to your God Within.*"

"I can't get up right now. Just let me stay here. I don't know if I want to live another day like this. I don't know, God. Is there a God? Is there only unhappiness? I feel so awful. I have to stop drinking. I must look after myself. Mom didn't fall apart after dad left. Mom flourished after dad left. I love flowers. I would have a room of flowers. Fresh flowers each day to bring happiness, to bring love. Love is always given with flowers. Weddings and funerals, flowers are given with love."

"*Listen to your heart's desire, Sweet One. Listen to the nudge of life. Listen to your purpose.*"

"What if I opened a flower shop? Mom, we would be surrounded by flowers. A big window for people passing by on the street to admire the flowers. I could give flowers to people feeling unhappy. I could give flowers to people feeling just like I do... empty. I wonder what his bride had for flowers? I wonder who put the bouquet together? I love making bouquets. I love flowers."

"Flowers are the gift to the earth."

"My life would be so different now, if only I would have ended the marriage before he did. I would feel better. I would have done better. I would have known better. Should have, should have. Could have, could have. Didn't."

"Gentle. Gentle with yourself."

"Why don't I just pick up the pieces? Why can't I live as though I left him? Why can't I move on with dignity and grace? He won. I lost. Why can't I be a good sport about it?"

"Gentle, Sweet One. You have within all your answers. All your guidance to live fully. To live authentically."

"Who would I be today if I chose something better for myself? Who would I be if I was more like my mom? Who would I be if I never met the man? Who would I be without my father leaving? Who would I be without the heartache and disappointment? Who would I be?"

"*You have the answers, Sweet One. Find your authentic self.*"

"Perhaps today, I turn it all around. Perhaps today, I can see the good that all the heartache brought. Right now, I can't move. My body hurts. My mind is spinning. My head hurts. Mom, do you know how I am feeling? Do the heavens know to come and help when help is needed? Did you really leave me, mom?"

"*Gentle. You are never alone. You are always connected to Divine Creation. You are always part and piece of the whole. You are whole.*"

"Maybe something to eat. Perhaps some toast. Mom always gave me toast when I was feeling sad about something. I guess toast reminds me of home. I miss my childhood, well, most of it. I had such big dreams. Dreams, where do they go? Do they just dissolve? Does time run out? Why do we not live in our dreams? Why does life take our dreams away?"

"*Your dreams are part of, never lost, never*

forgotten. Bring forth your Inner Essence of your Divine God Within."

"If I go back to where it all went wrong, where would I go? To what age? When did I not see the big picture? When did I decide to stop taking care of myself? I got so depressed when all the fighting started. I got caught up in the fighting, not the mending. I got used to the chaos and destruction. I got caught up believing that I was someone less than I am."

"*Sweet One, keep listening. Know of your brilliance. Know of your magnificence.*"

"Why did I let things get so out of hand? When did I let things get so out of hand? I saw the signs. I knew he wouldn't be faithful. I guess I gave him reason and an excuse to be unfaithful. But was it me, or is it his character? He wasn't so good to me and he knew it. He knew that I took his BS in times it wasn't even for me. I wonder if his new young bride is putting up with his BS, his lies, his deceit. She must realize that he will cheat on her. I suppose if she is a good wife and does the opposite of what I did, he will be faithful. I guess it isn't my problem now."

"Search within. Search for your Divine Inner Essence of Grace. Search for compassion."

"I must feel better soon. I think I took many wrong roads. Many roads that lead me to here. Here, lying on my bed suffering with a hangover. No job, no husband, nothing good to call my own. I have this home. Thank God, I kept this home. Thank goodness my mom helped me buy this home, and thank goodness, he knew enough to know to leave it with me. I gave him his money, he gave me the house, and as I look back, I guess, like my mom, he gave me my freedom. Freedom, what does that look like? Is it suffering in the middle of the day, not wanting to see the day, not wanting to get up, not wanting to look after myself? What have I done with my life? What have I done with my life?"

"Listen carefully. Your life is created. You choose every moment of your creation."

"How did I get to here?"

"Here is perfect. Here is now. Go forth, Sweet One. Go forth in your brilliance. Go forth with your life experience of contrast."

"I wish I had more friends. I haven't done anything to have friends. My former co-workers, they became life I suppose. I kept my distance, but I did enjoy their company when I felt so lost and miserable. I lied to them. They didn't know how I was really feeling. They didn't know how I was living, am living. God, do you know? Do you really see all? And if you see all, why can't it change? Why so much misery? Why, God, did you set life up like this?"

"Listen to your heart. You are the creator with free will. You choose with your free will."

"If I was going to play God for a day... what would I do? What would I change? I would change mankind. I would stop all war. I would stop people from killing people. I would stop hatred. I would stop the judgement and the condemnation. I would stop all hurt and fear. I would stop pain and suffering. I would stop all things that feel so awful. Why did all this happen to me? Why me? Why?"

"Sweet One, listen. Listen to your answers to your questions. You are brilliant. You are filled with wisdom. All souls are."

"If I was God for the day, I would stop poverty. I would stop starvation. I would stop cruelty and abuse."

"Listen to your words. Listen gently. Listen to your answers."

"If I was going to be God for the day, what would I choose?"

"You are part and piece of Divine. Search for your God Within."

"Okay, God. How does it work? What do I do to play God for the day?"

"Answer the questions you have just asked."

"Is it possible to stop the hurt, the pain, the suffering? Is it possible to stop war? Is it possible to teach others to stop being cruel and unkind, to stop killing mankind? Is it possible, God, that the world could be at peace?"

"Look within, Sweet One. Look within. It starts there. You have free will to choose."

"Listen to me. I can't get out of bed, and now I am going to play the role of God. Who do I think I am? I can't look after myself."

"Search within for your own peace. Search within to stop your own war within."

"If I was God for a day, truly, I wouldn't know where to start. Maybe, that is why God just leaves us to ruin the earth and mankind. Where would I start? God, where are you? Why can't you fix any of this? Why can't you fix this mess of life we live?"

"Listen, Sweet One. Listen to your own Wisdom of Grace. Listen to your own answers to your own questions."

"If I was God, I would change the world. I would change my world. What would I ask God for? If I was God, would I help my ex-husband? God can't choose who to help. I guess people do. God would love everyone. 'God is Love' as they say. I just don't understand why we don't feel it. Why do things feel opposite to love?"

"Love is who you are. Search within to your God Within. To your Love Within."

"God, where would you start with me, just me? Where would you start to make my life better? What a challenge... even for God."

"Listen to your Divine Inner Essence. Listen to your answers. We are One with Divine."

"I guess you would start by me getting out of bed. Perhaps, you would make me look after myself. Can God make anyone do anything? God, I guess you couldn't make me do something. I would have to do it with my own free will. Interesting. I am asking God for things that I would change with my own choices. God, is this why you don't help the suffering?"

"Listen, Sweet One. There is no condemnation in Divine Order. There is no judgement upon any soul."

"God, do you like being God? It must be hard to be God. Everyone wanting something from you. Everyone praying that you will hear them. How can you hear everyone? Some don't even believe in you. God, it can't be easy being you."

"You are Divine Inner Essence in the Great Light of All."

"God, why did you make me? Why am I here? Why didn't I just stay where I was? Where was I? Where was I before here? My head is spinning. Good question. I wonder what the answer is?"

"Listen for your answers. Listen to the gentle and loving whisper of your Divine Wisdom."

"Mom, do you know where I was before here? Where are you, mom? Are you in the same place you were before here? Where are you? Can you hear me, mom? Mom, can you hear me? God, can you hear me?

"There is that knocking again. What is that? I'm not getting up to check. It's probably those kids.

"Mom, do you like heaven? Is there a heaven? Is heaven where we are before here? Mom, I want to see you. I am so sorry you left without me having the chance to say goodbye. Mom, why did you have to die suddenly? Couldn't you have given me some kind of warning? Mom, why mom?"

"Held within your Divine Wisdom are your answers. Go searching for your answers."

"Mom, what does heaven look like? Is God there? I don't think he is here. I don't think you are here. I am alone. I am suffering on my own.

"What is that knocking?

"I can't get up. I don't want to get up. They will go away."

"*Gentle, Sweet One. Listen to your Divine Inner Essence. Hear the guidance for you. Feel the love for you. Listen tenderly as tender presence is holding you*."

"Mom, if there is a heaven, and you can come back, could you come and let me know you are here? Could you, mom, make your way back to here, even if you are an angel, or light, or whatever happens in the heavens? What are you now, mom? What are you now? Are you there? Are you still my mom? How does it all work? Why did you leave me so soon?"

"*Be gentle with yourself and see beyond what you know to be. Open your mind and your heart to the receiving of all the answers you are searching for. The answers are held within. Your Divine God Within*."

"Why are they still knocking? Okay, I am getting up. This better be good. This better be an emergency. What am I saying? I don't need an emergency. Grow up."

"*Listen to the guidance. Follow your heart that is speaking with you.*"

"There isn't anyone at the door. There isn't anyone here but me. Why do I keep hearing the knock? There isn't anyone there."

"*Quiet your mind. Open the receiving to your heart.*"

"Why am I hearing knocking? Every time I am asking my mom for something, I get interrupted with someone knocking, getting me up. My bed is so comfy. If I catch the brats that have found a way to knock on my door, God help me when I get a hold of them.

"Good, it stopped. I can't see anyone. I don't understand.

"Mom, who is knocking on the door? Mom, can you hear me?

"There it is again.

"Mom, who is it? There isn't anyone there. Am I losing my mind? Am I going crazy like the old crazy lady down the street? Mom, are you there?

"Mom, can you hear me? Mom... "

"*Listen, Sweet One. Hear beyond what you can believe to be.*"

"What is wrong with me? I am asking for my mom. Asking God to give me a sign. Asking my mom to give me a sign and all I get is this bloody knocking. All I get, is the sound of the clocks ticking, and knocking when no one is there."

"*Listen to your own words.*"

"Mom... God... Anyone?

"Mom! God! Anyone!

"I am alone.

"I am going back to bed. My head hurts, my heart hurts, I am broken. I feel the pain of life. Mom must love the heavens, no pain there."

"*Quiet your mind, Sweet One. Quiet your mind. Listen to your answers given.*"

"Why is it that when I call for my mom, stupid kids knock on the door? They must think I am the crazy lady. Kids always pick on the crazy lady. I should get myself thirty cats. I love my bed. I will stay here all day. I should eat. I am too tired to eat."

"Nourish your body. Nourish your soul. Comfort yourself with love."

"It can't be... it just can't be. I asked for a sign, and the knock was at the door. I asked my mom to speak to me, to let me know that I am not alone, and there was a knock on the door with nobody there.

"Mom... are you knocking? Is that possible, mom? Mom... is it you?

"I am losing my mind. I am losing my mind. Why not? I've lost everything else. Why not my mind?"

"Gentle... gentle... Feel beyond what you know. Seek within for the guidance. Seek within for who you truly are."

"Mom... is there a God? You should know, being in the heavens and all. Is it all Divine? Is it all that it is meant to be? Are you happy there, mom? Is there a place for me with you?"

"Quiet your mind. Quiet your mind..."

"Mom, I wish you were here. Maybe you are. Maybe, just maybe, a real long shot that you did knock for me, where would I look for you? You aren't standing in the doorway. Where do I look for you?"

"In your heart, Sweet One. Look Within."

"I have to sleep. I need to sleep. I can't sleep. What if it was you, mom, that could, in fact, knock? What would I say? What would I do?"

"Quiet to hear the whisper of love. Quiet your mind."

"Deep breath. Just breathe. Just breathe. Just breathe."

"Quiet. Gentle. Gentle. Quiet. Ease. Love. Grace."

"Mom, where are you? You must be an angel to come and look for me. Did you knock, mom? Did you knock?

"If you are here, what would you say to me as I lay here wallowing in my misery? I know... I can hear your voice. You would be saying, 'Get up. Time to start new. Time to start fresh.

Get up, brush your teeth, comb your hair and feel alive.' "

"*Feel deep within, Sweet One.*"

"Then you would tell me as we sat having a quiet cup of coffee, you would say, 'You have lost your job and in the loss you are to find something greater. In the loss, you are to find something that you are passionate about.' I know, mom. I know. You would say those exact words."

"*Listen to your guidance talk with you. Be gentle. Bring forth your love.*"

"Then as we laughed that my shoes need a three-inch heel, you would ask me... 'What do you wish for yourself?' You always asked that question. You always asked me that question. 'What do you wish for yourself?' I remember being five years old, crying, because I didn't get my own way, and you sat me down, looked me straight in the eye, and asked me... 'What do you wish for yourself?' Which I replied the thing I didn't have, and you said, 'It is yours, find it another way. Find it another way.' I then realized, that all you wanted was for me to ask for what I was wanting instead of my temper tantrum. Goodness, I was a handful... and you, mom, were the best mom."

"Listen. Hear your own wisdom speak through you."

"What do I wish for myself? Mom, I guess I wish to get out of bed and live a normal life. I wish happiness for myself, and love for myself... to myself. Mom, I wish you were here for myself, but you are not. I want to think that you are. Find another way. Mom, have you found another way? Are you here with me?"

"Feel your heart, Sweet One. Feel your heart."

"Mom, I want you to be here. I want to talk with you. You could tell me what I should do. You would say, 'What do you wish for yourself?' and I would reply, happiness. Then you would say, 'Then create happiness,' and I would reply, I don't know how. Not now, not for a long while. I just don't know where to look."

"Look within, Sweet One. Look within to your Divine Within."

"Mom, I would wish that I had my own

business, and that I flourished in my own business. I know, you would say, 'Then do it. Have your heart's desire.' You would make it seem so easy. You would encourage me and tell me to follow my dreams. Why did you die so young when you had such wisdom and passion for life? You knew life, mom. You knew what made others happy and sad. Today, mom, I am sad."

"*Listen to the whisper of gentle guidance. It is love in its purest form.*"

"Mom, you would say, 'Follow your dreams; they are for you.' Did you have all your dreams, mom? Did you complete everything you wanted? Is that why you left so soon, so suddenly? Did God need you more than I did? Does God need anyone? I bet heaven is a better place with you there."

"*You are One with Divine. You are One with the Heavens.*"

"Where would I find the strength to open my business? Where would I find the money, the time? Would I even know what to do? I see it clearly. Since I was kid, I wanted to be a florist. People said that I should find the corporate road. More money in that, they said. I did neglect what I truly wanted. Is that where I went wrong?"

"*This is the only moment to create.*"

"Okay, so now I am without a job, lying in bed with a severe hangover, talking to God and my dead mother... What is it all about? Why am I here? Why am I here?"

"*Quiet. Quiet. You are magnificent. Gentle with yourself. Start in this moment.*"

"Mom, you did leave me some money. I know you would want me to have my own flower shop. You would say, 'Take the money, spend the money, you can't take it with you, dear.' You didn't take it with you, mom. You left it with me. All your hard work, and you left me the money. How do I honour you?"

"*Listen. You are hearing the guidance from within. Listen, it is a whisper.*"

"Mom, why can't I see things like you saw things? You always could see the good among the tragedy. The good in people. The good in mankind. You saw the good in the challenges and the heartache. Mom, why... why can't I be like you?"

"*You are here for grand reason and great purpose. You are here to share your love.*"

"Mom, I wish we could open the shop together. We could have, but I was so caught up in someone else's dreams. I let my husband make the decisions. I wanted this nice house, so I worked hard, but I worked hard at a job I didn't like. I worked hard for someone else's business. Mom, I followed the rules of so-called life. I followed the pathway that we are all taught to take. Mom, I didn't have the confidence to open the business. I leaned on something that felt that it wouldn't collapse. And look now, mom. The whole thing has collapsed around my feet."

"*Now is the only moment.*"

"Mom, do you think I could? Do you think it is possible, mom, to have my business that I always wanted? Is losing my job a gift? Mom, you would say, 'Get up. Start. No time like the present moment.' You lived your life like that, mom. You lived in the moment, free of burdens. You didn't care about tomorrow. You would say it wasn't here to care about. You didn't worry about yesterday. You would say, it isn't there to worry about. The present is the gift, you would say. The present is the gift. Open the gift, you would say. Why didn't I take all this great advice while you were here? While I lived life to the beat of my own drum, I didn't listen to your wisdom. I am ready now, mom, to listen. Show me what is possible. Show me how to change every aspect of my life. Show me, mom, how I can live fully and happily. Show me how to live in peace and contentment. Stop crying. Stop crying. It feels like truth. For the first time in years, I can feel my own truth."

"Listen. You are guided in the Oneness, in the Wholeness, in the Vastness. You are held with loving care. Listen to your heart. Listen to your own wisdom of truth."

"For the first time, I feel excited about something. I haven't felt this way for years. What if it was possible? What if I could make my wish... reality? What am I thinking? I'm not there. I can't even get out of bed."

"Gentle. You are magnificent. Share your brilliance."

"Deep breath. Deep breath. Follow your dreams, mom would say. Follow your dreams. Perhaps, my husband followed his. Perhaps, mom followed hers. Perhaps, she wanted to go to the heavens because she did fulfill all her dreams in this lifetime. Maybe, just maybe, there is a reason beyond what I know that she left me. Maybe, just maybe, there is a reason beyond what I know that he left me. Mom left me a gift of her wisdom and all she shared. She left me knowing that I could see the world like she did. He left me knowing that I didn't see the world like she did. What if I could change it? What if him leaving was the perfect gift? What if all this heartache and trouble was for me to take a good look at me? What if I needed the change, and it took all this to make me see it? What if all this stopped my drinking? What if all this stopped the pain and suffering of beating myself up every day? What if mom was right? What if there is only this moment for me? If I was God, what would I do now?"

"Deep within I am here. Your Inner Essence to guide you. See your Light of Grace. See your brilliance and love. Bring forth love to

oneself. Bring forth love to all. For we are One with All."

"For the first time, I feel excited. I feel alive. I hurt, but I feel like something could matter. That my life could matter. What if I got my life together? What if mom is here? What if there is a God? What would I do knowing that my mom is helping me and that I am One with God? What would I do? What would I achieve? Where would I go? What would I give to others? I don't want to be a victim anymore. My mom would never have painted herself as a victim of anything. She knew she made all her choices, even if they didn't go her way. She always felt the path chosen would bring her to where she was meant to go. What if I was meant to go right to here? What if I could turn it all around? What if I could change?"

"*You are the creator with Divine Creation. You are part and piece of the whole. Listen to your guidance of love. The purest love for oneself is always the answer. Love is always the answer.*"

"The sun is shining. There is still half the day

to see. I should shower. I will shower. I should eat. I will eat. I should clean. I will clean. I should get my life together. I will get my life together. I should be kind to myself. I will be kind to myself. I should love me so much more than I do. I will love me so much more than I do. I should open the florist shop. I will open the florist shop. I should get a dog to love. I will get a dog to love. I should never look back. I will never look back.

"Mom, thank you for being right here. Thank you for showing me the way.

"God, thank you for not judging. Thank you for not condemning. God, thank you for all your love."

"*You have found me. You have found me. You have found your Divine Inner Essence of the purest love. You have found yourself.*

"*The truth is... you are magnificent.*"

God Bless

*Bring Heaven to Earth ~
and Earth Will
Be Your Heaven*

~ Love is the Answer ~
Love is Always the Answer

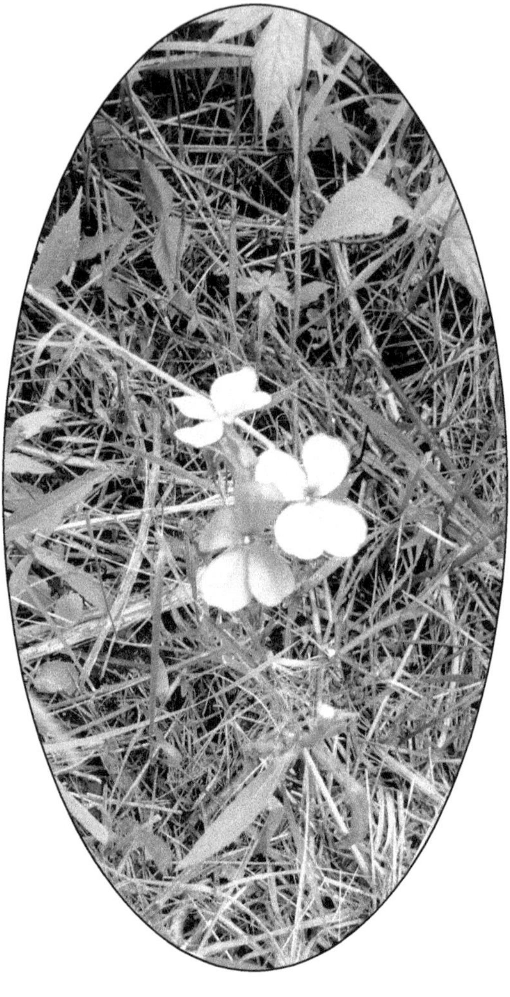

The journey of life – what is it all about – steps upon Mother Earth to create – the journey of life to bring forth the greatest part of you – for underneath layers of human experience is a love so grand it is light – your journey upon Mother Earth is to search and discover who you truly are underneath the layers of emotions – of setbacks and hurdles – underneath the judgement and condemnation – the hatred and the fear – your light is as pure as the light of the heavens – bring the Light of Divine Heaven to Divine Mother Earth and become all you are meant to be – walk your journey with love leading the way and know of your magnificence to share as One.

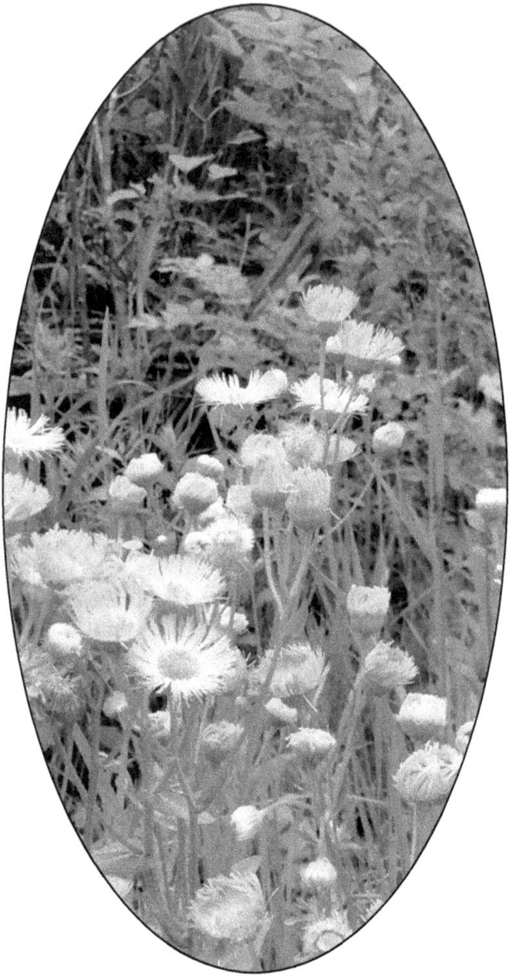

In the early hours of the morning while the stars still are seen in the darkened sky – when the sun is just about to emerge into the grandest glory of life itself – you are held in the light that shines upon you – you are held in the light that shines for you – for a new day emerges into all its Divine Glory for you – shine your Light of Divine Brilliance – shine forth to others as the sun shines life for all – held in the new day is your wisdom to bring forth your Inner Essence of Loving Light – for held with the stars that wait until the nighttime sky is your grandness and magnificence to shine for life itself – go forth in light – go forth in grand love – go forth and know that you are a miracle among the magnificence of all miracles.

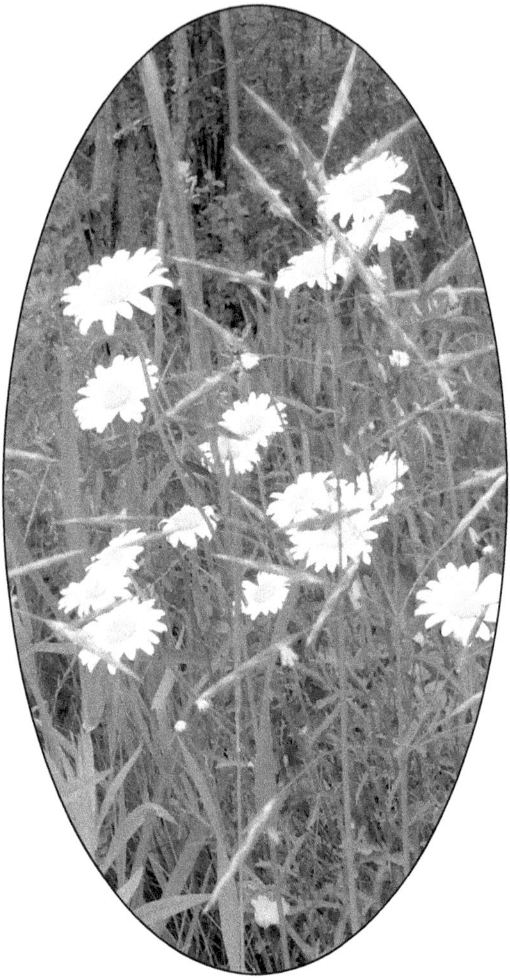

What does it mean to become all you are meant to be – with life experience it is easy to forget who you truly are – for you are a gift among miracles – beauty and Divine Grace – you are here for grand reason and great purpose – how does one remember this among the confusion of life – how does one bring forth Divine Inner Essence of the purest love among travels of disharmony – upset – war within and war among – it is a search – a desire to remember who you truly are – it is the knowing of your love held within – in order to bring forth great compassion and wisdom – how do you live in the purest love you are – is to know – is to be – is to become – is to love.

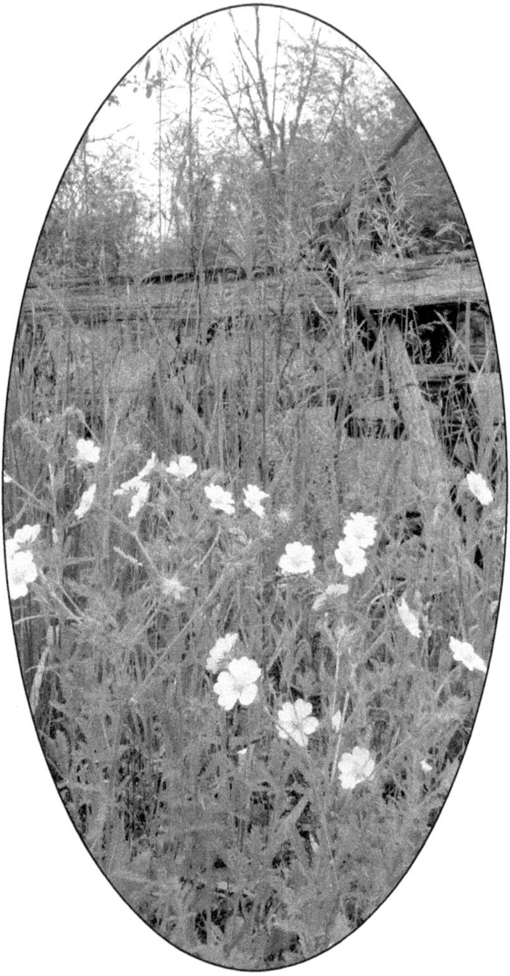

The gift of a new day – endless possibilities to share the best of who you are – to share compassion and love – to share joy and comfort – for even during the darkest days compassion can be felt – kindness can be shared – for in the days of sorrow lives within love to bring forth – the days of challenges and setbacks – frustration and anger – is held the beauty of your soul to bring forth your authentic self – for underneath life experience is who you truly are – the you that is One in the Oneness of all Divine – this day bring forth your greatest understanding of compassion and allow the day to show you miracles – for you are One with All.

Lightning Source UK Ltd.
Milton Keynes UK
UKHW012315280219
338228UK00010B/276/P

9 780368 338557